T0392240

Phoenix Rising

Felon Smith

ISBN: Softcover 978-1-9845-2255-9
EBook 978-1-9845-2254-2

This is a work of fiction. Names, characters, places and incidents either are the product of the author's imagination or are used fictitiously, and any resemblance to any actual persons, living or dead, events, or locales is entirely coincidental.

Print information available on the last page

Rev. date: 04/23/2018

To order additional copies of this book, contact:
Xlibris
1-888-795-4274
www.Xlibris.com
Orders@Xlibris.com

Phoenix
Rising
Felon Smith

Dedication

I would like to dedicate this book to the creator first. For doing something through me I could not do alone. I would like to dedicate this to my children kyla, Chloe, Sincere who inspire me to be greater for them and me and the world. I would like to dedicate this to any one who as been betrayed and still found a way to love and move on in life. To the underdogs of the world that has been cast aside, for if God be for you what man can be against you. The underdogs shall rise to any ocassion because they were made in the fire, like the phoenix. Selfishness and hate, greed, and jealousy can't change the world only love and cooporation can.

A special thanks to my Big Sister Brandy Martin aka Big Redd entertainment for being there for me and my children through the Good,the Bad,and the ugly. I love you.

I would like to give a special thanks to my dad Willie Smith gone but not forgot – My ship has finally come.

Also I would like to give thanks to my three moms in this life Jorgetta Martin, Florence Smith, Diane Nicholson R.i.P

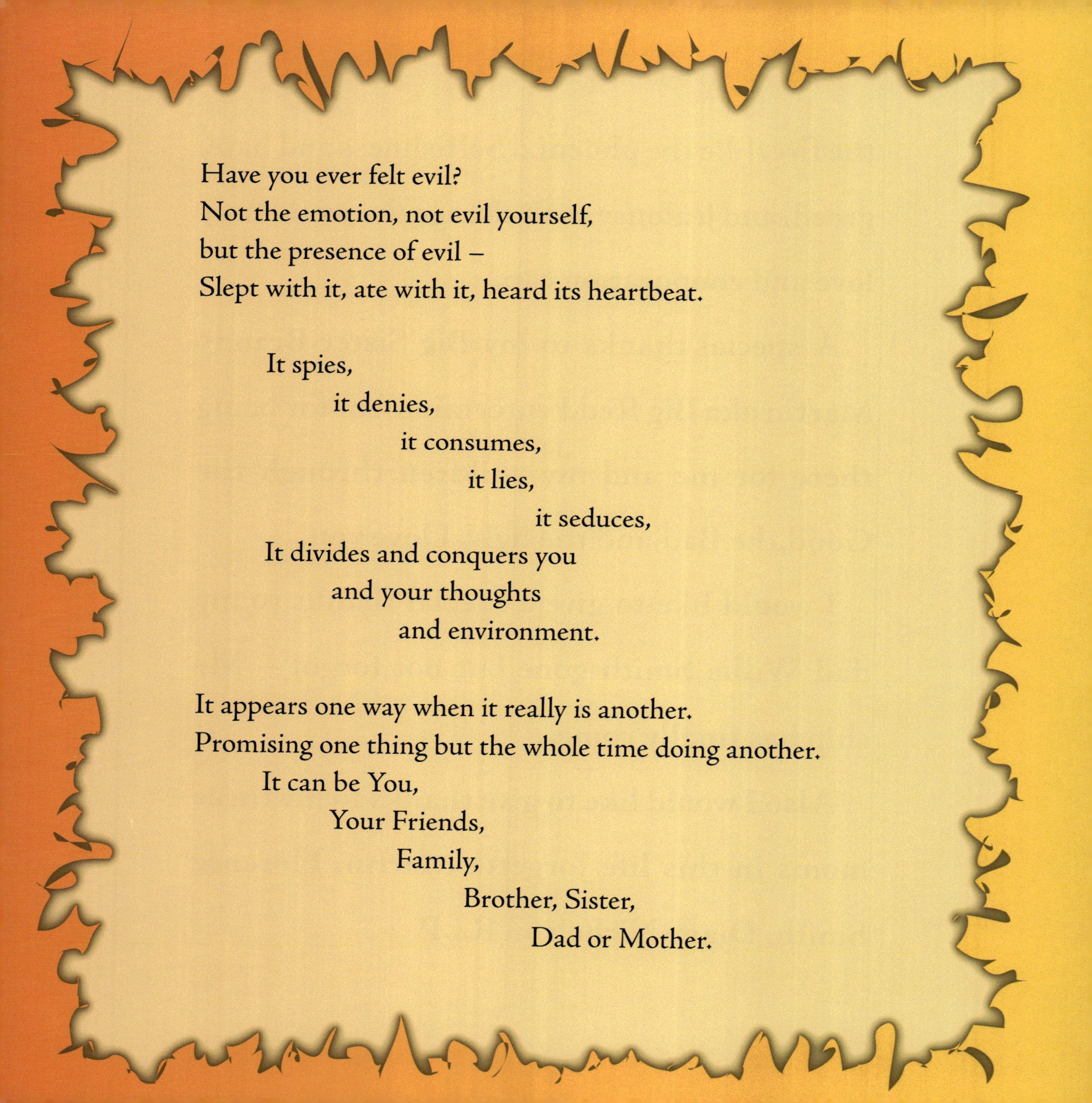

Have you ever felt evil?
Not the emotion, not evil yourself,
but the presence of evil –
Slept with it, ate with it, heard its heartbeat.

It spies,
it denies,
it consumes,
it lies,
it seduces,
It divides and conquers you
and your thoughts
and environment.

It appears one way when it really is another.
Promising one thing but the whole time doing another.
It can be You,
Your Friends,
Family,
Brother, Sister,
Dad or Mother.

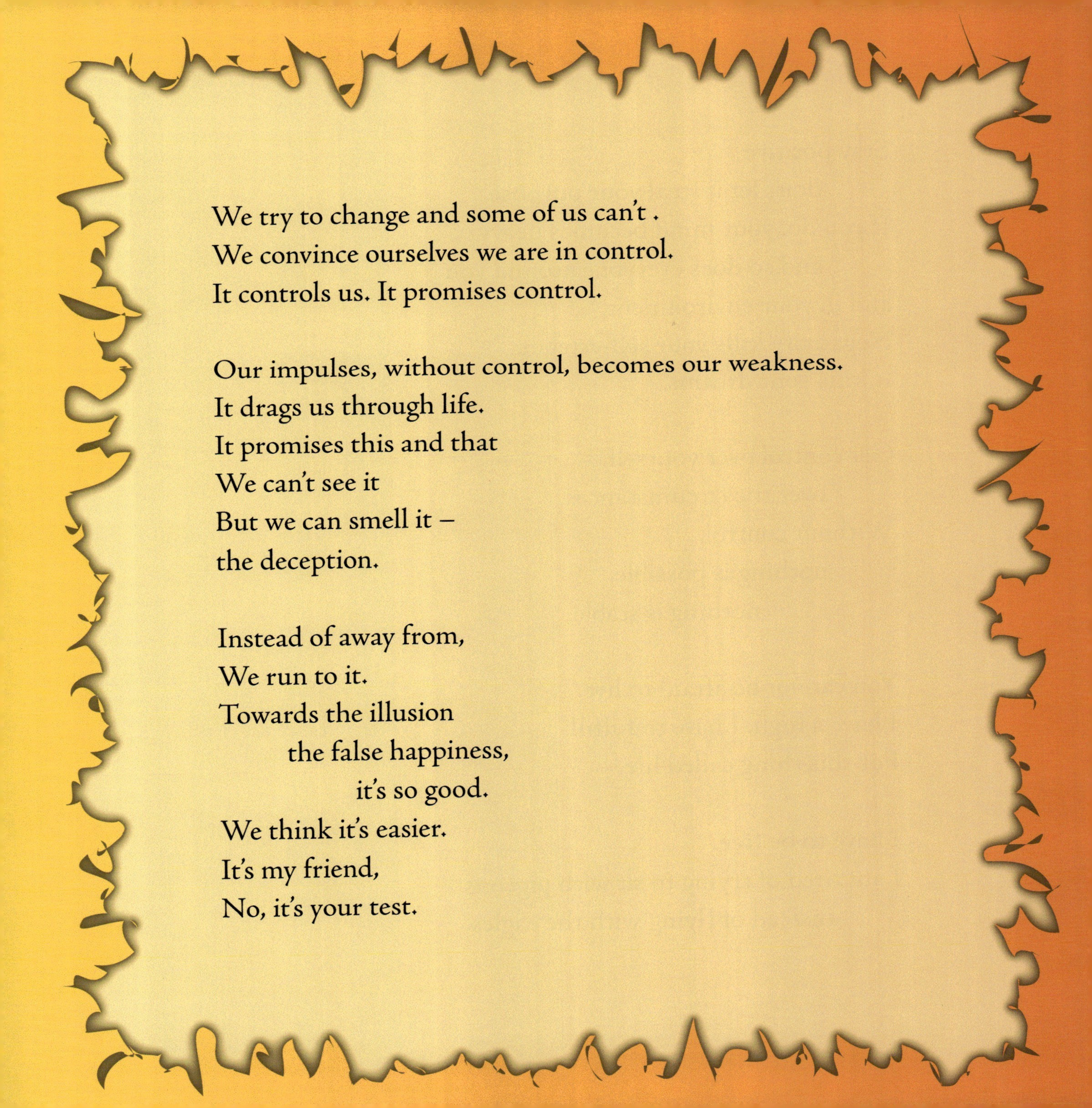

We try to change and some of us can't .
We convince ourselves we are in control.
It controls us. It promises control.

Our impulses, without control, becomes our weakness.
It drags us through life.
It promises this and that
We can't see it
But we can smell it –
the deception.

Instead of away from,
We run to it.
Towards the illusion
the false happiness,
it's so good.
We think it's easier.
It's my friend,
No, it's your test.

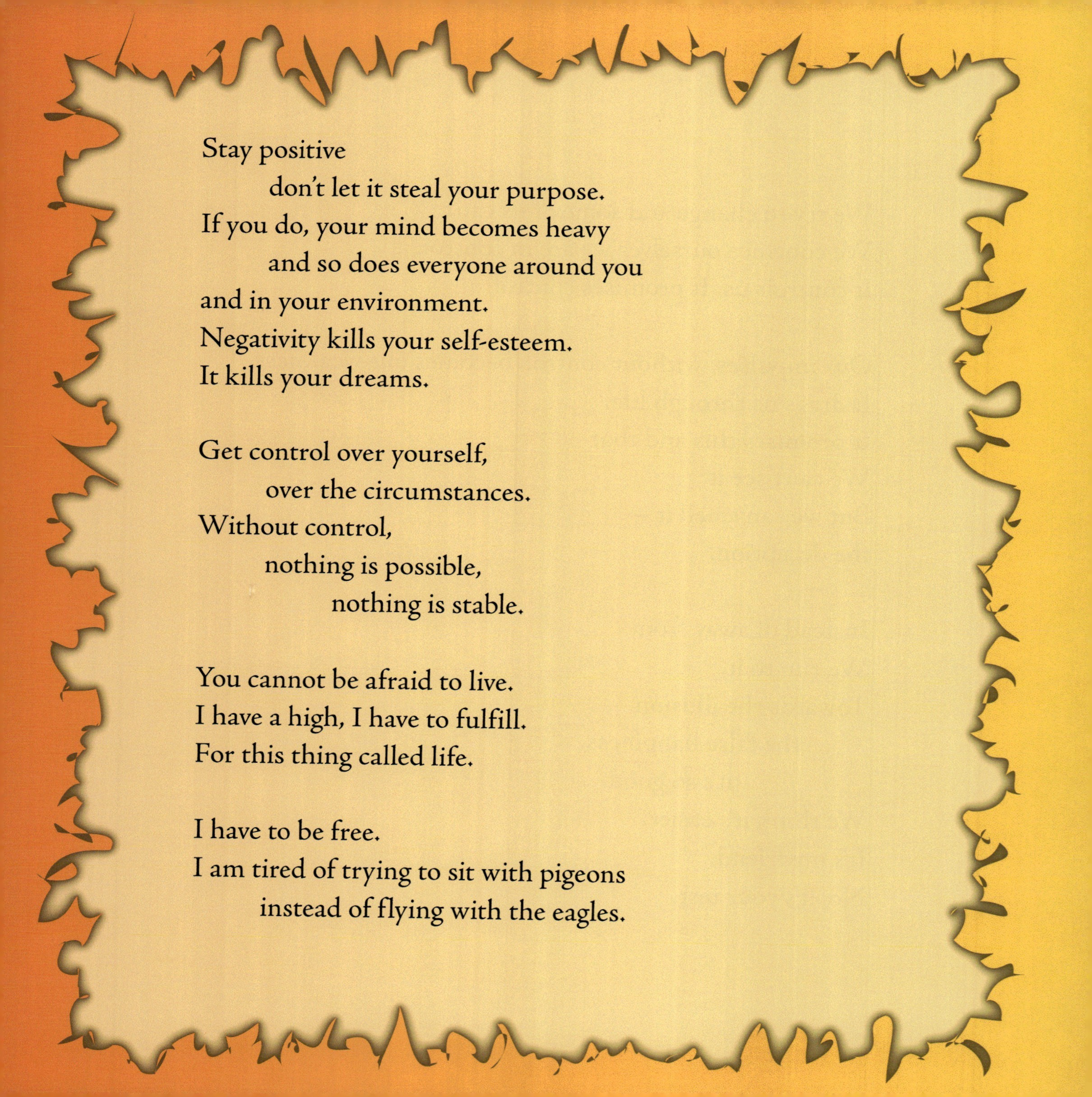

Stay positive
don't let it steal your purpose.
If you do, your mind becomes heavy
and so does everyone around you
and in your environment.
Negativity kills your self-esteem.
It kills your dreams.

Get control over yourself,
over the circumstances.
Without control,
nothing is possible,
nothing is stable.

You cannot be afraid to live.
I have a high, I have to fulfill.
For this thing called life.

I have to be free.
I am tired of trying to sit with pigeons
instead of flying with the eagles.

I am an Eagle.

I am a winner,
I have to be with winners,
I was born to win.

What were you born to do?

Some people give too much.
I realized I gave too much to undeserving people,
but the universe gives back to those of us that deserves it.

Smiles, I realized I have a limitless supply of talent.
I am made in His image.
No one can take everything from me,
hold me responsible for their mistakes.
While breaking down,
you built me up
and I'm still building.
Here I come walking in these shoes.
I am not afraid anymore, I don't believe your lies anymore.
Don't be scared now.

I won't share:

Not my dreams with evil.
Not my love, not my destiny,
Not my family and my future.

We are all both good and bad
but some more than others.
My self-respect is the cost,
damn if I was gonna sell out,
it wouldn't be for a few pieces of silver.
My soul's not for sale.
They say we all have a price, do we?
They will have drained,
losing all desire to win with all they take from you,
yet wonder why you're too depressed to win.
I have to get control over the situation.
I will love myself more than they hate me,
And I will win.

We all matter in this world.
When people think you don't matter
show them how indispensable you are.
It's sad when you're a rainbow
and a lot of people are color blind in this world.
They are from life trials and tribulations.

Do you know that some people are so ignorant?
Some people are so jealous,
that they don't realize that we all play a part in this game
called life.
What they want?
They want you to waste your life with them. Lies.

Evil promises this and that.
We can't see it, but we can smell their deception.
We all do it.
Instead of away from, we run towards the illusion,
the false hope,
and happiness
it's so good.

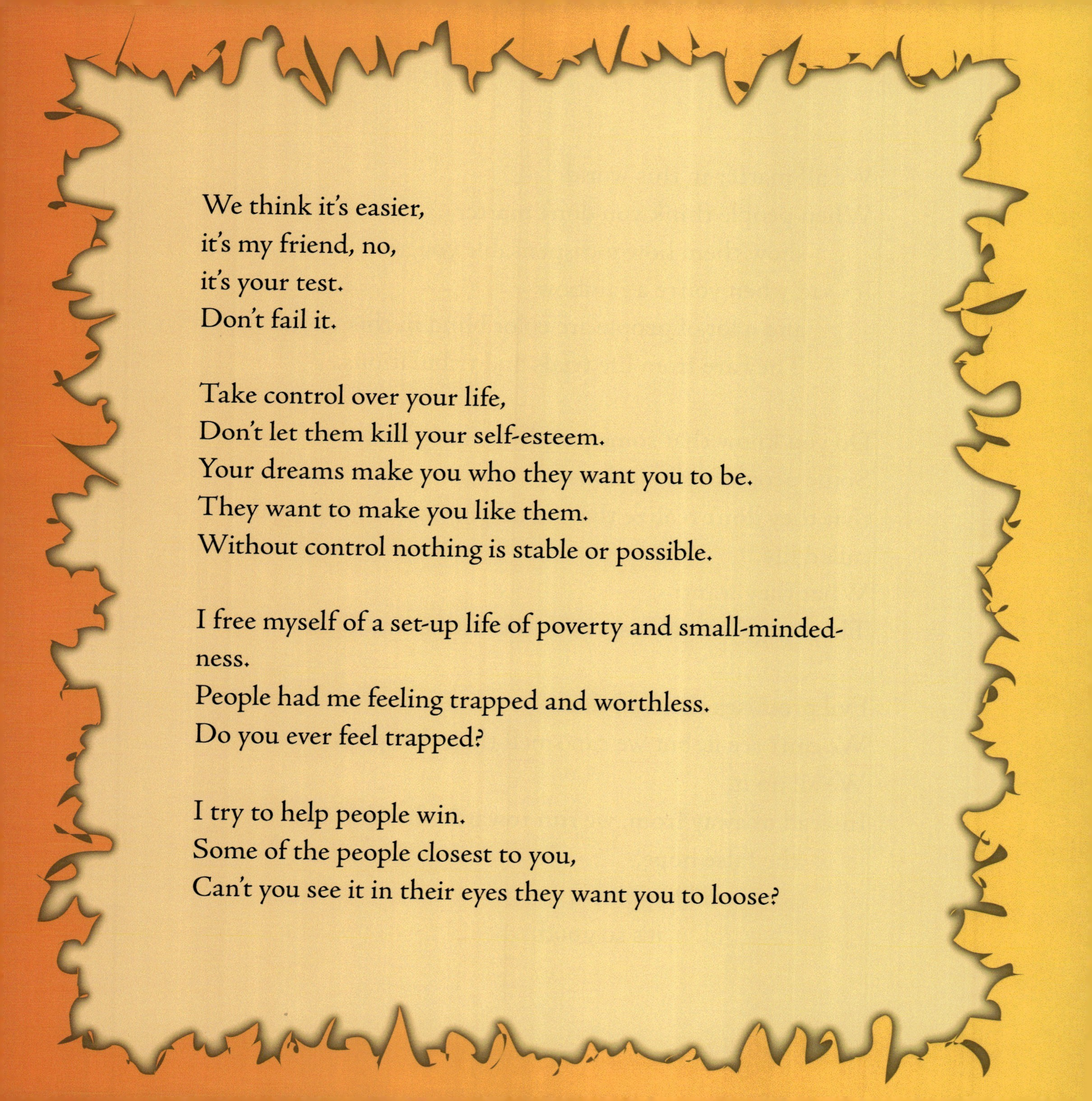

We think it's easier,
it's my friend, no,
it's your test.
Don't fail it.

Take control over your life,
Don't let them kill your self-esteem.
Your dreams make you who they want you to be.
They want to make you like them.
Without control nothing is stable or possible.

I free myself of a set-up life of poverty and small-minded-
ness.
People had me feeling trapped and worthless.
Do you ever feel trapped?

I try to help people win.
Some of the people closest to you,
Can't you see it in their eyes they want you to loose?

I have to fight daily for my morals and for my values.
I have to make them see me.
Fulfill me.
Show them some movements can't be stopped,
This is one. I fly amongst the greatest.
The men and women in this world
that conquered their fears.
I am tired of feeling out of place, do you?
As a People,
we all do and accept things
that make us feel helpless
and so out of place.
I am one of the ones who lived through the evil,
who merged with it for the greater good.

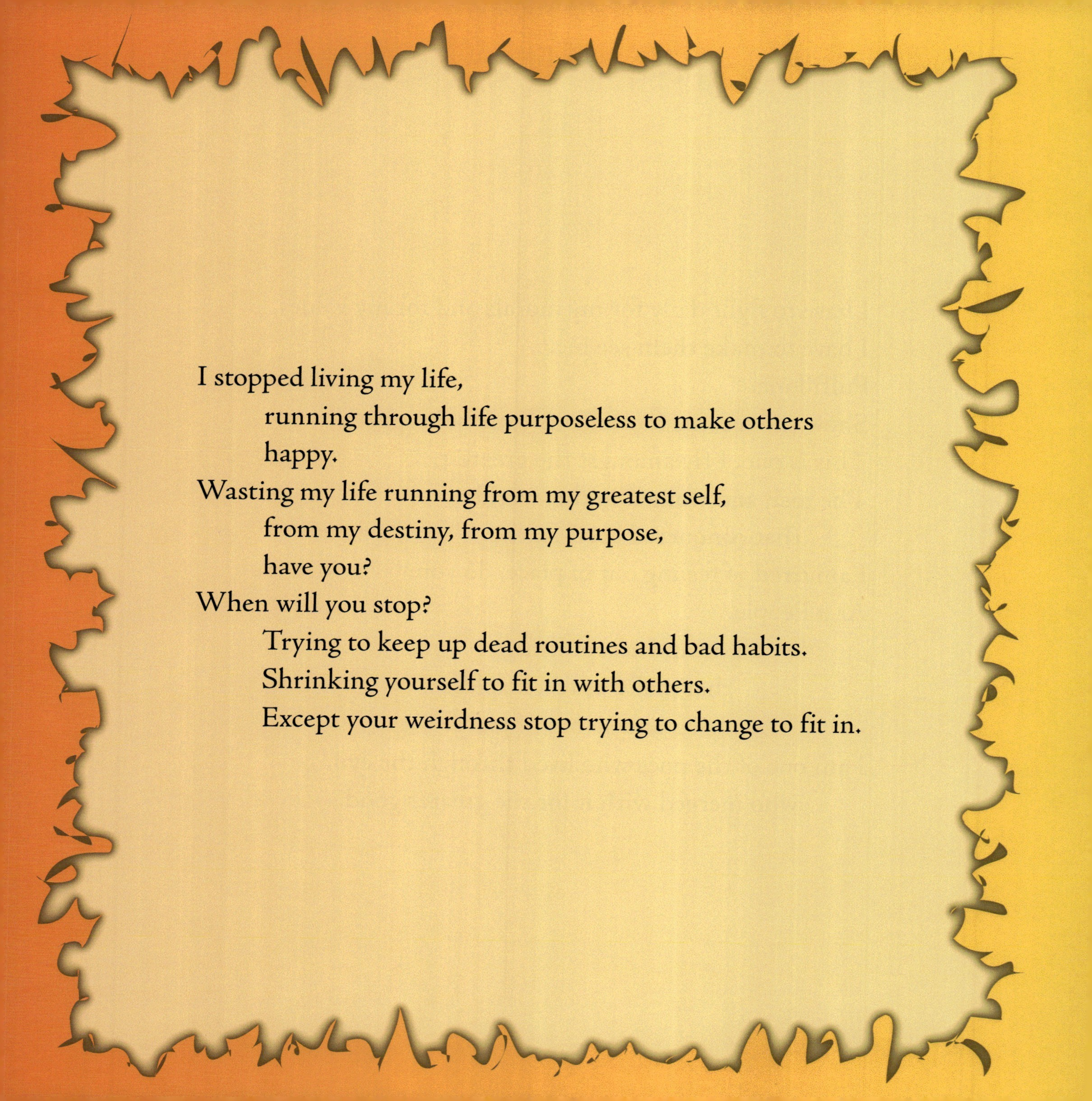

I stopped living my life,
running through life purposeless to make others happy.
Wasting my life running from my greatest self,
from my destiny, from my purpose,
have you?
When will you stop?
Trying to keep up dead routines and bad habits.
Shrinking yourself to fit in with others.
Except your weirdness stop trying to change to fit in.

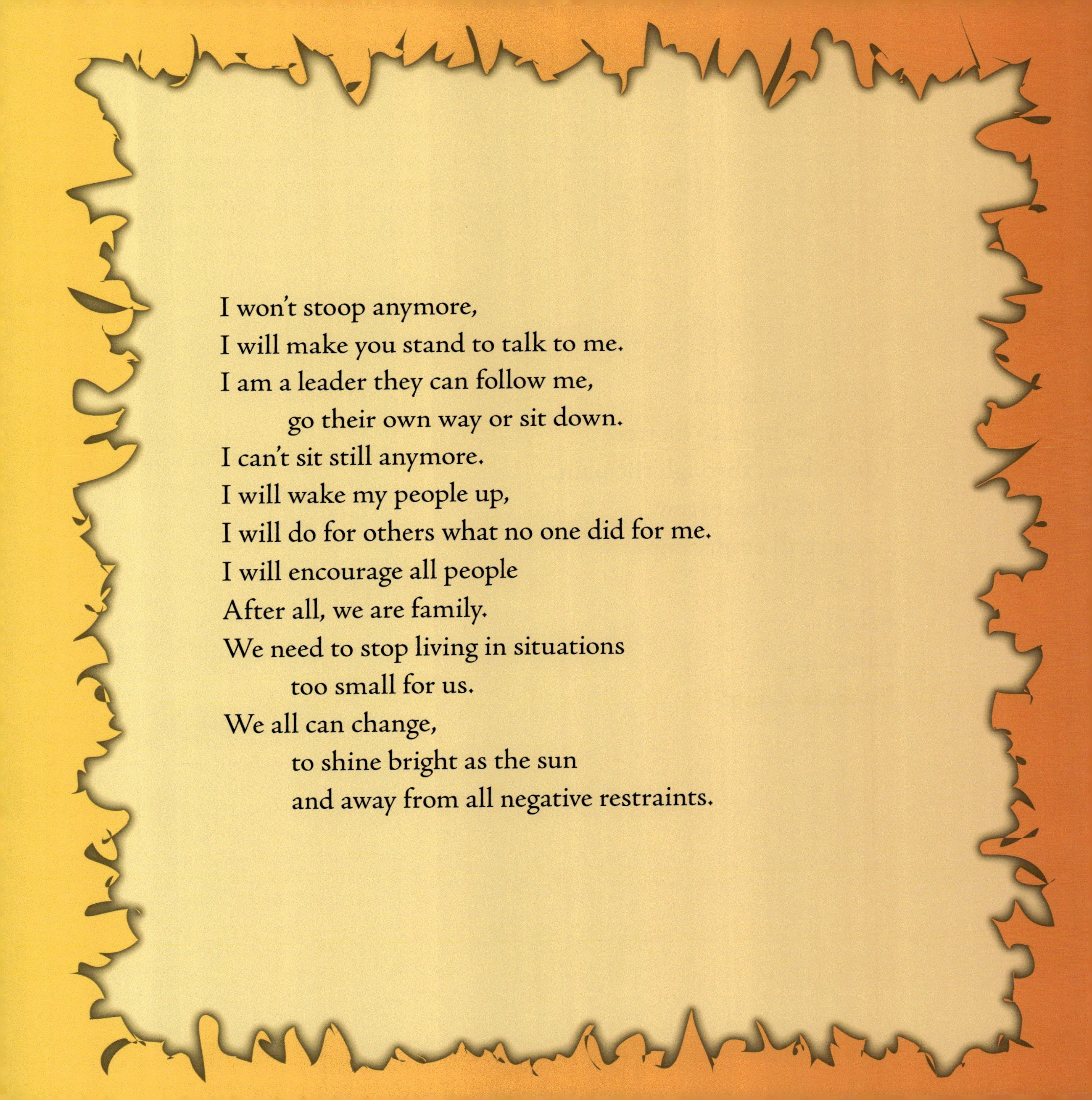

I won't stoop anymore,
I will make you stand to talk to me.
I am a leader they can follow me,
go their own way or sit down.
I can't sit still anymore.
I will wake my people up,
I will do for others what no one did for me.
I will encourage all people
After all, we are family.
We need to stop living in situations
too small for us.
We all can change,
to shine bright as the sun
and away from all negative restraints.

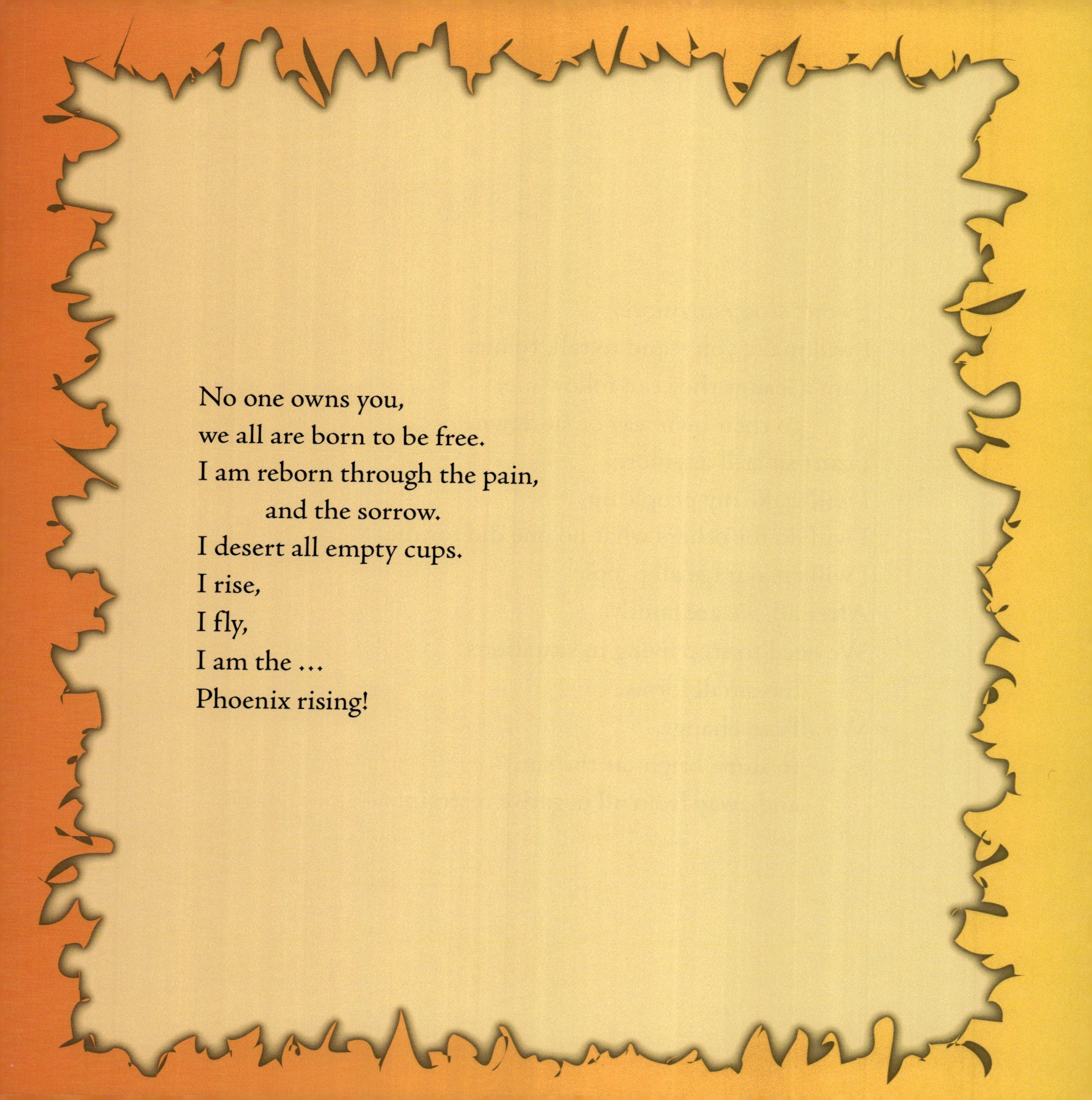

No one owns you,
we all are born to be free.
I am reborn through the pain,
and the sorrow.
I desert all empty cups.
I rise,
I fly,
I am the …
Phoenix rising!

Printed in the United States
By Bookmasters